JUMPY JACK & GOOGILY

& SOPHIE BLACKALL

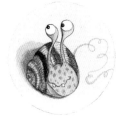

PUFFIN BOOKS

Published by the Penguin Group: London, New York, Australia, Canada, India, Ireland, New Zealand and South Africa
Penguin Books Ltd, Registered Offices: 80 Strand, London WC2R 0RL, England

puffinbooks.com

First published by Henry Holt and Company, LLC 2008
Published in Puffin Books 2009

002

Made and printed in China

ISBN: 978−0−141−50241−0

For glorious Gloria,
who thought this one up too

— M. R.

For Eggy and Lachlan, of course

— S. B.

"I'm nervous," said Jumpy Jack to his best friend, Googily. "There could be a monster nearby and I'm scared of monsters."

"Don't be ridiculous," said Googily.

"There might be a monster behind that tree," said Jumpy Jack.

"Now, now," said Googily. "You are very silly to worry."

"Perhaps I am," said Jumpy Jack.
"But I would be grateful if you would check,
just to be sure."

"No monsters here," said Googily.

"Or here."

"Phew," said Jumpy Jack.

"Uh-oh," said Jumpy Jack. "There might be a monster in the tool shed. It might have sharp teeth and horrible scary hair."

"I don't know where you get your ideas," said Googily.

"Nonetheless," said Jumpy Jack, "I would appreciate it if you would check, to be absolutely certain."

"No monsters here,"
said Googily.

"Phew," said Jumpy Jack.

"Oh my," said Jumpy Jack. "There might be a monster in that paddling pool. It might pop up all of a sudden and smile a dreadful smile or make bug eyes at me."

"Dear, oh dear," said Googily. "What an imagination you have!"

"All the same," said Jumpy Jack, "I would feel better if you would check, just to be safe."

"No monsters here," said Googily.

"Or here."

"Phew," said Jumpy Jack.

"What if there is a monster behind the door?" said Jumpy Jack. "What if there is a monster with two fingers on each hand, who stares at me through the letterbox and sticks out its awful tongue?"

"Oh, Jumpy Jack," said Googily. "You must realize that will never happen."

"Of course not," said Jumpy Jack. "But I would feel a great deal better if you would check, just in case."

"No monsters here," said Googily.

"Or here."

LETTERS

"Phew," said Jumpy Jack.

"**What if** there is a monster under the table?" said Jumpy Jack. "What if there is a monster with long thin feet that jumps out from under the table and frightens me so much **I** nearly faint?"

"Ho ho ho," said Googily. "Now you **really** have gone too far."

"Maybe so," said Jumpy Jack. "But if you would check, I would be extremely grateful."

"No monsters here," said Googily.

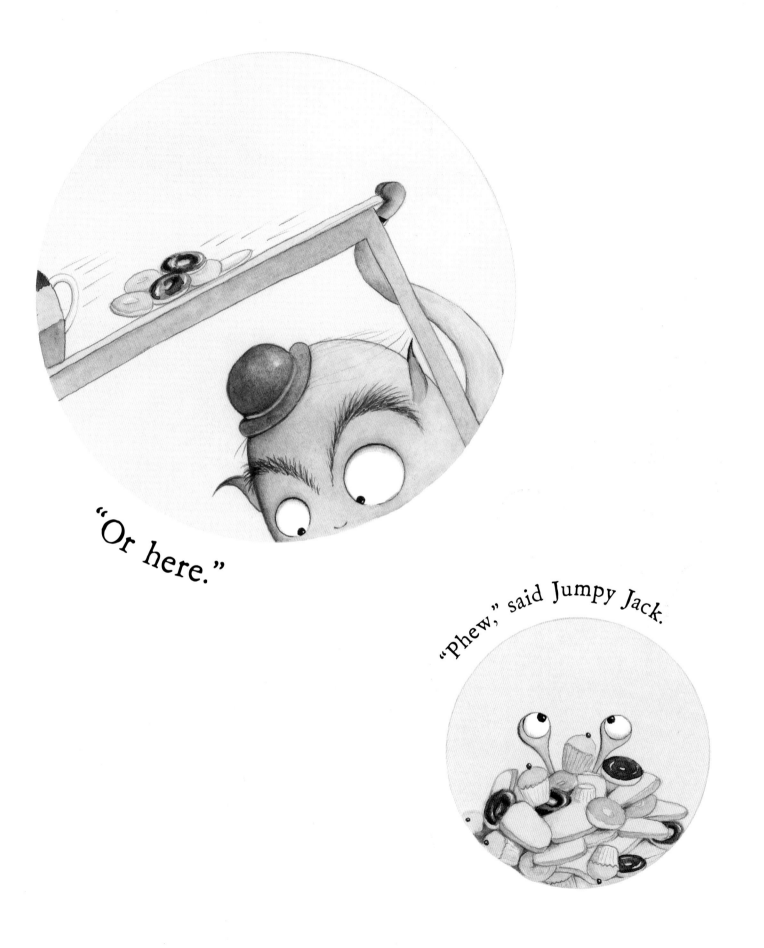

"Or here."

"Phew," said Jumpy Jack.

"**What if** there is a monster under the bed?"
said Jumpy Jack. "It might be wearing terrible short
trousers and a bowler hat, and wait until I'm almost
asleep, then leap out with an alarming tooth-grinding
noise and give me the most dreadful fright so I have
to climb out the window and run away like the wind."

"Jumpy Jack!" said Googily. "That is simply too far-fetched."

"No doubt," said Jumpy Jack. "Still, if you would only check, I'm sure I would sleep better."

"No monsters here," said Googily.

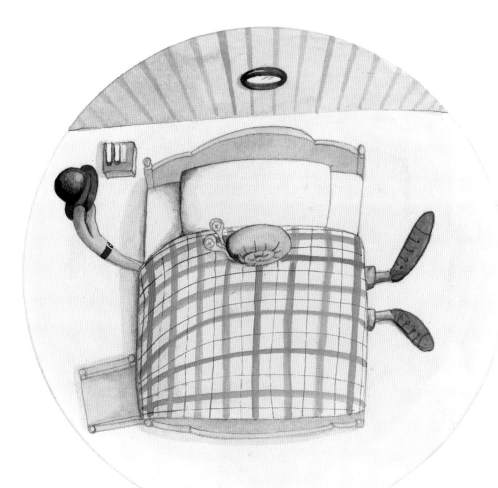

"Or here."

"Phew," said Jumpy Jack.

"Let's go to sleep."

"Jumpy Jack?" whispered Googily.
"I can't sleep."
"Why not?" asked Jumpy Jack.

"I thought I heard a sock under the bed. And I am **extremely** frightened of socks."

"Boo!" said the sock.